The
Pear
in the
Pear
Tree

For Jacob, Ashley and Thomas

Cnr Rosedale and Airborne Roads, Albany, Auckland, New Zealand
Penguin Books (South Africa) (Pty) Ltd
4 Pallinghurst Road, Parktown 2193, South Africa
First published by Penguin Books, 1999

1 3 5 7 9 10 8 6 4 2

Designed by Deborah Brash/Brash Design Pty Ltd, Sydney
Typeset in 26pt Weidemann Book by Brash Design Pty Ltd
Printed in Australia by Book Connection

National Library of Australia
Cataloguing-in-Publication data:

Allen, Pamela.
The pear in the pear tree.

ISBN 0 670 88316 6.

1. Title.

A821.3

Visit our website at www.penguin.com.au

The Pear in the Pear Tree

Pamela Allen

VIKING

When John and Jane went out walking,
they were busy talk, talk, talking.

Until ...

'Look,' said John. 'Look up there.
I can see a juicy pear.'

They couldn't reach. They had a try.
What will they do? It's up too high.

They fetched a ladder. 'I'm ready,' said Jane.
'You must hold it steady.'

But just as Jane was reaching out
poor John let out a warning shout.

The ladder *leaned*…
Jane *screamed*…

OOOOOWWWWWWWW!!!!!

Now clinging to the top-most rung,
just like a metronome she swung ...

back and forth, back and forth.

ooooow!

Soon John was running very fast
to keep Jane up. It didn't last –

Jane like a fishing lure was cast.

OOOOOOWWWWWWWW!!!!

SPLOSH!

A bird was sound asleep that day
in a pond not far away,
when Jane came hurtling from the sky
and landed SPLOSH-SH-SH nearby.

The startled bird got such a scare.
She was shot UP... in the air.

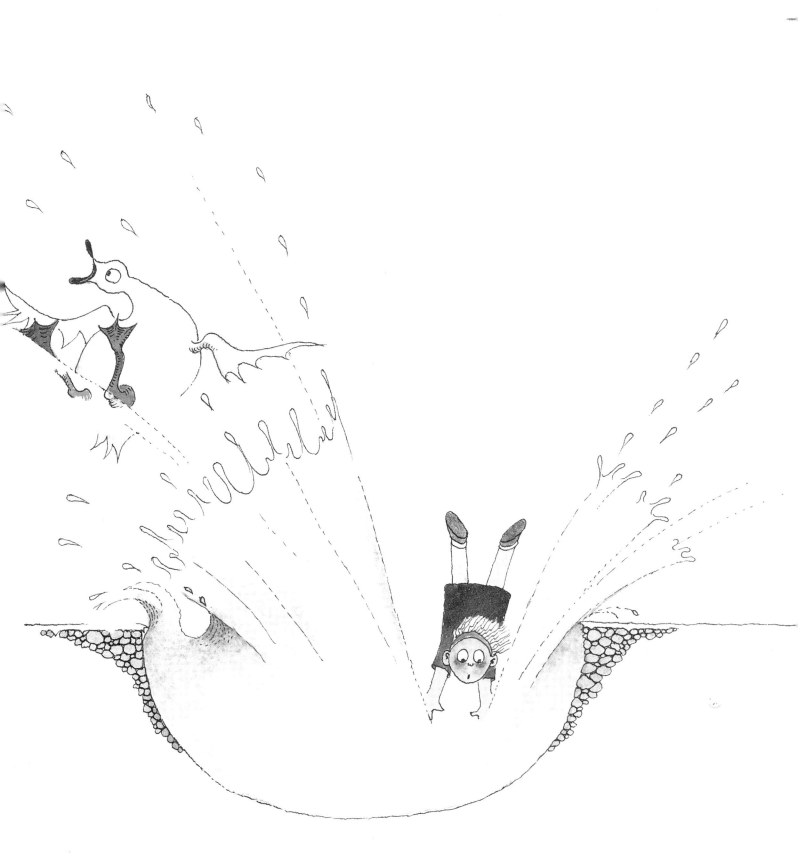

Jane was struggling in the water.

John reached out his hand and caught her.

Now Jane was wet with dripping hair,

but *still* they had to have that pear.

How will they *ever* reach up there?
How will they *ever* get that pear?

Boingng-ng ... the bird dropped from
the sky and landed on the branch, up high.

She landed PLONK! in quite a state
and bent the branch with her great weight.

Although she landed heavily,
and bounced and rocked unsteadily,

John was able to reach the pear
now that she was sitting there.

The pear was fastened very tight.
They pulled and pulled with all their might.

TWANG-NG! the precious pear came free.
And then the bird, as you can see,
was CAT-A-PUL-TED from the tree.

She landed SHHPLOP! back in the pond,
safe and sound where she belonged.

John and Jane now ate the pear.
One bite each – that was fair.
They ate it up, down to the core.
'That's all,' said Jane. 'There is no more.'